The "Granny" Who Wasn't Like Other Grannies

DENIS BOND

Illustrated by Valeria Petrone

Hippo Books
Scholastic Children's Books
London

Scholastic Children's Books,
Scholastic Publications Ltd,
7-9 Pratt Street, London NW1 0AE, UK

Scholastic Inc.,
730 Broadway, New York, NY 10003, USA

Scholastic Canada Ltd,
123 Newkirk Road, Richmond Hill,
Ontario, Canada L4C 3G5

Ashton Scholastic Pty Ltd,
PO Box 579, Gosford, New South Wales,
Australia

Ashton Scholastic Ltd
Private Bag 1, Penrose, Auckland
New Zealand

First published by Scholastic Publications Ltd, 1993

Text copyright © Denis Bond, 1993
Illustrations copyright © Valeria Petrone, 1993

ISBN 0 590 55133 7

Typeset by BWS Graphics

Printed by Proost International Book Production

10 9 8 7 6 5 4 3

Tim loved his granny, but sometimes
he wished she were like other grannies.
Other grannies did granny things, like
knitting and sewing and reading.
But not Tim's granny.

It wasn't using the old bed in the front garden as a trampoline that upset Tim. Although that was bad enough.

It wasn't even that she'd
go-carted across Mr Green's lawn
and churned up all his grass.
Tim had coped with that.

What had upset Tim most,
was when Granny had done
handstands in the High Street.
Passers-by had tutted and said,
with disgust, "Look at that granny!
She's showing her knickers!"
This had made Tim go red.

"I'll have a word with her today," said Tim. "I'll invite her to tea. Then I'll ask her to behave like other grannies." Granny arrived, as usual, on her motorbike. BRRMM…BRRMM…BRRMM! POP…POP…POP!

"Oh, dear. She's so noisy," sighed Tim.
"Hey! Look!" Tim's friends laughed,
as they pointed at Granny's bike.
"Grannies don't ride motorbikes," they said.

"This one does!" smiled Tim's granny.

Before Tim had a chance to say anything,
Granny dragged him off to the park, to
watch the football match.
She rattled her football-rattle and
jumped up and down and cheered.
Tim tried to pretend he wasn't with her.

Before long, Granny had joined the players on the pitch. She kicked the ball much *much* harder than anyone else. "YES!" everyone shouted, as Granny scored the winning goal.

The footballers lifted her up and chanted:
"WE ARE THE CHAMPIONS!"
Granny chanted along with them.
Tim looked around to see if anyone he knew
was watching.

Then Granny remembered the fairground
on the far side of the park.

"I love fairgrounds!" she yelled
and she raced across the field
towards the bright lights.
"Wait for me, Granny!"
Tim called as he chased after her.

FIRSTLY...
Granny sped round and round the
bumper-car track, smashing into all
the other cars.
BIFF! CRASH! CLUNK!
All the other drivers were terrified.
Tim was quite frightened too.

THEN . . .
"Faster! Faster!" screeched Granny,
as she hurtled down the big-dipper.

Other grannies watched her and tutted.
"Grannies don't ride on big-dippers,"
they said. "Grannies stand and watch!"

FINALLY...
All the other grannies and their grandchildren screamed as their carriages on the ghost-train brushed past the spiders and the skeletons and the ghosts. But Tim's granny just laughed.

And she pulled such an ugly face, that she frightened away all the ghosts.

Later, Granny took Tim to the adventure playground. There were frames to climb on and ropes to swing from.
Other grannies watched as their grandchildren played. But not Tim's granny. She climbed higher than any of the children.

"WHEEE!" she screamed as she swung on a rope from one side of the playground to the other.
"Look what she's doing!" tutted the other grannies. "At *her* age! It's disgraceful!"

Suddenly it began to rain and all the grannies wrapped their grandchildren in raincoats and hats and wellington boots.
But not Tim's granny.
She danced around in the rain until her hair was limp and her clothes were sopping wet.

"Let's jump puddles!" she giggled.
Tim wasn't very keen. "I think it's time
we went home," he said. "I'm very wet."
But Granny leapt into a huge puddle,
soaking everyone from head to toe.

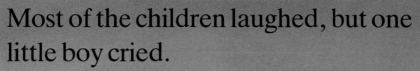

Most of the children laughed, but one
little boy cried.
"You've made me all wet!" he bawled.
"Oh, shut up!" said Granny. "Don't be such
a cry-baby."

All the other grannies gathered around her,
shaking their fists, angrily.
"Clear off!" they said. "You're a disgrace to
grannies!"
Tim's face went bright red.
It often did when he was with Granny.

When they reached the bus-stop, Tim
was very quiet. Granny knew that he
wanted to say something to her.
And she thought she knew what it was.

As the bus trundled back home, Granny said, "Do you wish I were more like other grannies, Tim?"
Tim looked at the other grannies on the bus.
"Sometimes," he replied, softly.
"Then I'll try," she said. "I'll try very hard."

The next day, all Tim's friends were waiting, excitedly for Granny to arrive on her motorbike. She wasn't like their own grannies, but she was fun to be with.
"Where is she, Tim?" they asked.
"Why hasn't she come?"

Tim was worried, so he went to
Granny's house. He found her sitting
in a rocking-chair, doing some knitting.
"I'll make you a cup of tea in a minute,
Tim," she said quietly. "And then
we can do a jigsaw-puzzle together."

Tim was disappointed as he wanted
Granny to play a game of *he* with him
in the garden.
He was about to tell her this, when he
realised she was fast asleep; snoring loudly.

And Tim remembered all the silly things that his granny had done. And it made him smile.

"I liked you better as you were before,"
whispered Tim. "I don't want an ordinary
granny. I want my special granny."
Granny leapt up from her rocking-chair
and cartwheeled across the room.
"I hoped you'd say that!" she laughed.

Granny reached behind the sofa for a box.
"This is for you, Tim," she said.
I wonder what's in it? he thought.

Inside, there was a pair of shiny, new
roller-skates.
"Oh, smashing!" gasped Tim. "I've always
wanted a pair of roller-skates."
"Me too," winked Granny as she opened
another box and took out a pair of
roller-skates for herself.

31

That afternoon Tim skated round and round Granny's garden.
GRANNY skated round and round her garden, too. "You may not be like other grannies," laughed Tim. "But I don't care. I love you just the way you are."